Suddenly Tracker had a horrible feeling he knew exactly what the man had been after!

With an outraged yelp, the beagle puppy rushed into the back room again, and straight over to the huge refrigerator. Standing up on his hind legs, he stared at the top of the door. . . .

"It's gone!" Tracker barked.

"What's gone?" Sheena asked him.

"The recipe for the bake-off!"

Other books in the

ALL-AMERICAN PUPPIES *Series by*

Susan Saunders

ALL-AMERICAN PUPPIES

6

THE BAKE-OFF BURGLAR

Susan Saunders

Illustrated by Henry Cole

AVON BOOKS

An Imprint of HarperCollins*Publishers*

Library of Congress Catalog Card Number: 00-109640
ISBN 0-06-447307-4

First Avon edition, 2001

❖

Visit us on the World Wide Web!
www.harperchildrens.com

THE BAKE-OFF BURGLAR

Tracker was patrolling the back room at the Main Street Bakery that morning. A reddish brown and white beagle puppy with a large black patch on his back, black edging on his long ears, and black freckles on his tapered muzzle, he was making sure everything was just as it should be.

He trotted up and down the aisles, sniffing at each large bag of sugar and flour and cornmeal.

Tracker's humans, the Pearsons, hadn't opened the bakery for business that day. Instead, they'd driven into the city right

1

after breakfast to pick up a new electric mixer. They'd left Tracker in charge while they were gone, a job that he took very seriously.

He peered under the huge stove where the Pearsons did all of their baking. Not a single crumb spoiled the spotless floor.

The shiny steel refrigerator hummed briskly, crammed full of eggs, butter, and cream. Stuck to the front of it was the recipe that Mr. Pearson had been working on for weeks, for a cherry-chocolate-chip angel food cake.

Tracker's humans were hoping to bring home another grand-prize trophy from the York County Food Fair and Bake-Off. They'd won it four years in a row.

Mr. Pearson had been saying, "It's getting harder and harder for us to come up with a brand-new championship recipe."

But Tracker was sure they could do it again.

He breathed in the rich scents wafting

from the spice racks: cinnamon and nutmeg and ginger . . .

The beagle puppy sneezed—ginger always made him sneeze.

"Sssssh!" someone hissed from behind a large sack of walnuts.

A fat, furry orange cat lifted his head to scowl at Tracker. "I'm trying to get some shut-eye!" Puffy said sleepily.

A second orange cat, Mr. Purr, was stretched out on the counter next to the sink. He looked almost exactly like Puffy, except that he had a couple of black whiskers in the middle of his white ones.

And the two cats smelled completely different, of course. Mr. Purr smelled like dusty old catnip, while Puffy smelled more like the Pearsons' coat closet.

"You've already sniffed at every inch of this shop at least ten times!" Mr. Purr growled down at the beagle puppy. "So give us a break: knock it off!"

"You two should be guarding against

mice!" Tracker told the cats sternly. "That old building across the parking lot is being torn down, and it's *full* of mice. Where do you think they'd rather move? Into a shoe

store?" Scott's Shoe Repair was two shops over. "Or into a bakery?"

To the beagle puppy, the answer was clear. But Mr. Purr said, "What kind of mouse

would want to share space with two ferocious cats?"

He pulled his lips away from his sharp white fangs in a dangerous grin.

"A really *dumb* mouse, if you ask me," said Puffy, flicking his striped tail.

Suddenly there was a loud woof outside the back door of the bakery.

"I never thought I'd be glad to hear from *them!*" Mr. Purr said to Puffy.

Them meant Tracker's four best friends: Jake, Rosie, Sheena, and Fritz. The five puppies spent most of their mornings together, exploring the town of Buxton from one end to the other.

But today Tracker couldn't go with them—he had the bakery to watch over.

He hurried to the dog door and slid through it.

Four puppies were waiting for him on the back steps, ears pricked.

"Ready?" said Jake, a tall,

mostly black Lab with a white-tipped tail that was always wagging.

"We're going to the lake!" said Sheena, a long-haired dachshund puppy.

Sheena was half Jake's size, but she had enough energy for a Great Dane.

Jake continued, "First we'll swim, and then we'll—"

"Chase water rats!" said Rosie, a bristly gray puppy with funny-colored eyes.

Rosie was born in the city, but now she lived in Buxton with John from John's Deli.

Fritz murmured, "Okay with you, Tracker?"

Fritz usually let the others make his plans for him. The German shepherd was the largest puppy of the group. He was also the youngest, and his ears hinted at

his timid frame of mind: his left ear tried to stand up bravely, while the right one sagged limply sideways.

"I can't do it, guys," Tracker told them all. "The Pearsons drove into the city. So I'm keeping an eye on things here. And a nose, too."

"Not even for a little while? We don't have to go all the way to the lake," Sheena said.

"We can run over to the park and wade in the duck pond," Rosie suggested.

A striped orange head with two black whiskers poked through the dog door: it was Mr. Purr.

Jake, Sheena, Rosie, and Fritz barked a few times, because they always barked at the bakery cats. And the cats always hissed at them.

When Mr. Purr finished hissing, he said, "Do me a favor—give Tracker a long walk."

"But I can't . . ." Tracker began.

"Puffy and I have everything under control," Mr. Purr said, yawning widely.

"Well . . ." Tracker glanced around the parking lot behind the Main Street Bakery. It was empty except for a couple of Dumpsters piled with boards from the old building that was being torn down. The beagle puppy raised his head to sniff the air—nothing unusual drifted past his nose. There really didn't seem to be anything for him to worry about.

"Okay," Tracker said at last, hopping off the back steps. "But only for a little while."

"Great!" said his friends, jumping down, too.

"It has to be all five of us, or it's just no good," Sheena added as they set out for the park.

CHAPTER TWO

The town park was a few blocks away from the bakery, on Fresh Pond Lane.

The park had a playground for little kids, with slides, seesaws, sandboxes, and swings.

Past the playground, a wide green lawn with plenty of room for running swept down to a small pond.

The lawn was dotted with huge trees that were home to several families of frisky squirrels. The pond was always crowded with noisy ducks and geese. The park was a pocket-sized puppy paradise.

Tracker, Jake, Sheena, Rosie, and Fritz

trotted quickly through the playground. They were careful to sidestep a toddler just learning to walk, and another flinging sand out of a sandbox.

On the green lawn beyond it, two boys tossed a Frisbee back and forth.

Sheena yapped excitedly, and Jake wagged his tail so fast that it blurred: What was better than big kids with a Frisbee to throw?

A tall boy with yellow hair said, "Wow— a whole team of pups."

"You guys want to chase this Frisbee?" his friend said to them.

"You bet!" Tracker barked.

All five puppies raced after the Frisbee as it sailed through the air. It got hung up in a bush, and Tracker reached it first—he jumped high to grab the Frisbee with his teeth.

Jake, Sheena, Rosie, and Fritz galloped after him as he carried it proudly back to the humans.

The two boys threw the Frisbee for the puppies until each of them had retrieved it once or twice.

Then the game was over. The boys climbed onto their bikes and rode away. The puppies walked down to the pond, hot but satisfied.

Rosie bounded into the water, splashing a trio of quacking ducks.

Jake was a great swimmer: He swam straight out to the middle of the pond.

Everything except his nose, the top of his head, and the white tip of his tail was underwater.

Sheena didn't like getting her long hair wet. She waded close to the shoreline, and Fritz waded with her.

Tracker sat down in shallow water to cool off. He breathed deeply, pulling in smells of gooey mud, ducks and frogs, and damp dog fur.

He was glad he'd come.

The puppies hadn't been in Fresh Pond long, however, when Jake suddenly raised himself out of the water.

"Hey, Tracker!" he woofed. "Is that one of your cats headed this way?"

Tracker had never seen Puffy or Mr. Purr anywhere near the park. But one sniff told him it was Puffy, tearing across the lawn toward them.

Puffy's orange fur was standing on end, his green eyes were wide open and wild.

Had something happened at the bakery?

Tracker charged out of the pond to meet the cat. "What's wrong?" he yapped.

"Mr . . . . Purr!" Puffy gasped to catch his breath.

"What about Mr. Purr?" Jake ran out of the water, too.

"He's trapped in the back of a truck, and who knows where it's taking him!" Puffy wheezed.

His fat sides were heaving, his thick tail thrashed back and forth.

"But how did he . . . ?" Rosie and the others had joined them, too.

"This human . . . climbed . . . through the . . . window," Puffy huffed.

"At the bakery?" said Jake.

"I knew I shouldn't have left!" Tracker howled.

"Why did he climb through the window?" Sheena asked.

"Because the door was locked? *I* don't know why humans do what they do!" Puffy snarled. "Do you?"

15

He added in a lower voice, "I couldn't see well because I was sitting under the stove." Louder, Puffy said, "Anyway, he climbed right back out again. Mr. Purr followed him. And so did I, after a little while. The human hopped into a big truck, and . . . and that's when Mr. Purr jumped into it, too. And it drove away with him aboard!"

"If only I'd been doing my job . . . I have to get back!" Tracker barked.

He shook water out of his coat, then started running.

"I'm coming with you!" Jake was hard on his heels.

"Me too!" Sheena yipped.

"You'll need some backup!" yapped Rosie. "Shake a leg, Fritz."

"Wait for me!" Puffy yowled.

Tracker dashed across the green lawn, zigzagged through the playground, and sped down Fresh Pond Lane. The others weren't more than a couple of steps behind him.

The beagle puppy dodged squirrels, kids, even cars. His heart was pounding. Thoughts tumbled around in his mind.

Was the man who'd climbed through the window a burglar?

There was no money in the cash register, because the bakery was closed for the day.

So what could the burglar have stolen? Mr. Pearson's best tart pans? Mrs. Pearson's favorite whisk?

Tracker and his friends reached the parking lot in back of the bakery in no time.

Humans were already at work on the old building across the way. A half-dozen trucks were parked near the Dumpsters.

"Was it any of those trucks?" Tracker asked Puffy.

Puffy shook his head, too winded to answer out loud.

So Tracker dove through his dog door, into the back room of the bakery.

Jake, Sheena, and Rosie slipped through

the dog door as well.

Fritz was too big to fit through it easily, and he was frightened besides. Whimpering unhappily, he crouched on the steps.

So did Puffy, still spooked by the break-in.

But Tracker found the back room just as it was when he'd left. Everything seemed to be in its place.

"What did the Pearsons have that the man might have wanted?" Jake said.

Tracker was thinking out loud, "What about the bake-off trophies?"

The beagle used his nose to push open the swinging door into the front room. The other puppies hurried in, too.

But all four trophies gleamed near the window. There was just enough space left over on their special shelf for this year's award.

"I could use an almond croissant," Sheena murmured. She peered hopefully into the glass bakery case.

There were no croissants to be seen, or cranberry oatmeal cookies, either, because the Pearsons hadn't baked that morning.

The front room was dark, cool, and bare.

"Puffy said the human wasn't in the shop long, so he couldn't have grabbed much . . ." Rosie began.

Suddenly Tracker had a horrible feeling he knew exactly what the man had been after!

With an outraged yelp, the beagle puppy rushed into the back room again,

and straight over to the huge refrigerator. Standing up on his hind legs, he stared at the top of the door . . . .

"It's gone!" Tracker barked.

"What's gone?" Sheena asked him.

"The recipe for the bake-off!" Tracker said. "That human climbed through the window and stole the cherry-chocolate-chip angel food cake recipe!"

"Bummer!" said Jake.

"It sounds scrumptious," said Sheena regretfully.

Rosie drooled a little, and licked her lips.

Tracker stuck his head through the dog door and woofed, "Puffy—get in here!"

CHAPTER THREE

"Okay, tell us again, fast!" Tracker said to the orange cat. "The human climbed through the corner window . . . ."

"What did he look like?" Jake asked Puffy.

"I don't know. I slid under the stove as soon as I heard the window rattling. I was taken by surprise, okay?" Puffy said crossly. "So I only saw his feet. He was wearing sneakers."

"So are about a zillion other humans," Rosie muttered.

"What did the man's feet do?" Tracker said.

"They walked over to the refrigerator," Puffy said.

"For the recipe," Tracker said grimly.

"A few heartbeats later, the man hurried to the window again," Puffy said. "He climbed through, and closed it. Mr. Purr scrambled out of wherever he was hiding. He jumped through the dog door . . . I got to the back steps in time to see a dark truck pulling out of the parking lot, with Mr. Purr trying to hang on in back!"

"Poor old cat," Sheena said kindly.

"He's brave enough. But he's not used to any rough stuff," Jake added.

Tracker was sniffing at the floor in front of the refrigerator. He could smell his own scent, he could smell the cats, he could smell Jake, Sheena, and Rosie . . . and he could smell new rubber! The human's sneakers were new . . .

The rubber smell led the beagle to the corner window.

"I'm tracking him," he murmured.

Tracker dashed to the dog door and dived through it, to pick up the rubber trail

on the other side of the window.

But it didn't take him far. At the edge of the parking lot, the scent trail disappeared altogether.

"I guess the human got into his truck right here," Tracker said, his heart sinking.

He sniffed the air.

It was full of human smells that came from the men tearing down the old building. There was no quick way that he could sort out the burglar's scent from the others.

"Mr. Purr put himself in great danger to help out the Pearsons!" Puffy growled. He didn't have to add, "Which was *your* job," because Tracker knew it.

The orange cat went on, "You're supposed to have such a terrific nose. So find him!"

"Of course—Mr. Purr!" Tracker exclaimed. He knew precisely how Mr. Purr smelled—he could track the cat!

And if Mr. Purr stayed in the truck to the end of the line, Tracker would also find the human who'd stolen the Pearsons' recipe!

The beagle puppy raised his head higher, and opened his mouth a little. Every trace of scent that surrounded him flowed into his nose.

Yes! The faint smell of dusty old catnip hung in the warm, still air. Tracker's tail started to wag.

"He's got it!" Tracker heard Jake say.

Beagle nose held high, Tracker followed Mr. Purr's scent across the parking lot, to the exit onto Oak Street.

Up Oak Street he went. The beagle was shadowed by four puppies and one fat orange cat, keeping their distance so as not to disturb him.

Tracker trailed Mr. Purr around the corner, onto Northville Road.

Northville Road pointed straight out of Buxton.

"If the truck headed out of town," Tracker mumbled, "I'll never find that recipe!"

And if I don't, I'll . . . I'll have to turn myself in at the animal shelter! the beagle vowed with

an aching heart. *Because I could never face the Pearsons again.*

Which made the beagle puppy trot faster and faster. The catnip smell grew stronger as he went.

He hurried past large houses with small yards, then small houses with big yards.

Strange dogs called out to him and his friends.

"Running away?" a gray-bearded collie woofed from behind a chain-link fence.

"Where's the fire?" yelped a dalmatian hooked to an overhead line.

"Open my gate, and I'll be your body-guard!" rumbled a lean Doberman with a spiky mouthful of teeth.

"Do we look crazy or something?" Rosie barked back at him. She was a city pup, and not easily frightened.

But Fritz whined and tucked his tail between his legs.

"You'd better be careful!" yapped a flouncy Pomeranian standing on a screened

porch. "Or Animal Control will scoop you up."

That was enough for Puffy.

"I'm out of here!" he meowed.

The fat orange cat slunk into a drainage pipe and disappeared—he was on his way home.

But Jake, Sheena, Rosie, and Fritz stuck with Tracker.

There weren't many houses left in Buxton now. Just a couple more cross streets, and the puppies would be putting the town behind them.

Suddenly Tracker couldn't smell Mr. Purr anymore. He couldn't smell anything but black coffee. And muffins: corn, bran, and whole wheat.

"Food!" Jake said, smelling them, too.

Just ahead, a small wooden building squatted on the opposite side of Northville Road. The sign on the roof had a giant muffin painted on it, along with a steaming mug of hot coffee.

"It's the Muffin Man," said Sheena. "I came here once with Heather for bran muffins." Heather was Sheena's human.

"Were they good?" Rosie asked her.

"Just plain muffins. Not half as good as the Pearsons' almond croissants," Sheena said.

"It's not open yet," said Jake. "And I'm starving."

He'd lived on the street for part of his short life, he'd gone without food—and he was permanently hungry.

"I wonder if there are any trash cans we can dig through?" said Rosie.

Before Tracker could stop them, first Rosie, then Jake and Sheena dashed across the blacktop and around the small building to the back.

Not Fritz, though. Or Tracker.

The beagle puppy took some deep breaths, hoping to pick up Mr. Purr's scent trail again.

But nothing could compete with the smell of coffee and muffins hanging over the Muffin Man.

So Tracker crossed the road, too, ready to scold his friends for letting their stomachs get in the way of duty.

Besides, he could use a quick snack himself, to keep his strength up.

CHAPTER FOUR

As soon as Tracker reached the far side of the road, however, several scents floated free from the heavy aromas of coffee and bran and oats.

The beagle puppy smelled dusty old catnip again.

He also smelled dried cherries, chocolate morsels, and vanilla beans—none of which went into plain muffins as far as he knew. But all of which went into the Pearsons' cherry-chocolate-chip angel food cake!

Had Tracker tracked down the recipe? And the burglar? If he found Mr. Purr, he'd know for sure!

The beagle trotted around the building.

A couple of overflowing trash cans leaned against the back wall, not far from a narrow door.

Rosie and Jake were pawing at the crumpled paper cups and napkins that littered the ground.

Even Sheena was picking through the mess, although she was being careful not to get herself dirty.

"Here's a chunk of oatmeal muffin," Jake said, nosing a plate aside. "Want some, Tracker?"

But Tracker's eyes—and his nose—were

focused on the dark truck parked beyond the puppies.

The smell of old catnip grew sharper and stronger as the beagle puppy walked silently forward. Was the orange cat hiding in the truck?

"Okay, Mr. Purr, you led me here," Tracker said when he was

close enough. "I owe you one. Now who's got that recipe?"

There was no answer from the feline.

The beagle puppy stood up on his hind legs and rested his front feet on the back bumper. He tried to look into the truck bed. But he was a bit too short.

Short, but nimble. Tracker could climb fences, even trees when he felt like it.

He galloped away from the truck. Then he whirled, ran straight at it . . . and threw himself at the tailgate. The beagle puppy hooked his front paws over the edge of it. Scrambling with his back feet and claws, he pulled himself up and over the tailgate, and tumbled onto the truck bed.

There was no Mr. Purr in sight; just a spare tire and a plastic tarp. But the smell of him was still so strong.

Tracker poked his nose under the tarp.

The tip of the beagle's nose brushed across a mound of dry fur. It was Mr. Purr, and, for once, he didn't hiss, or even

grumble. In fact, the cat didn't move.

"Find something?" Jake asked.

The mostly Lab puppy was a lot taller than Tracker, tall enough to see over the tailgate.

Fritz's head appeared beside Jake's. Both of his ears drooped, and he was whimpering—he was really scared. But he was sticking with his friends.

"I found Mr. Purr!" Tracker told them.

"I knew you would!" said Jake. "Your nose knows!"

"So what are we waiting for? Let's get out of here," Fritz whimpered.

"I'm still looking for the recipe. And Mr. Purr isn't going anywhere right now," said Tracker.

"Why not? Is he . . ." Fritz began fearfully.

"No, he's breathing," Tracker said.

The orange cat's sides raised and lowered slowly. But Mr. Purr's eyes were closed tightly, and he didn't open them, not even when Tracker poked him again with his sharp nose.

"He could have banged his head, rolling

around back here," Jake said.

"Maybe you could lick him awake!" Rosie was standing behind the taller pups.

"He'd hate that," Tracker said.

He was wondering what to do about the stunned cat when he heard a sound he knew very well.

The Pearsons had been using an electric mixer day in and day out at the Main Street Bakery—the angel food cake took an awful lot of mixing.

Now a mixer was whirring away inside the Muffin Man.

Tracker hopped up on the spare tire. Then he jumped onto the roof of the truck. He was high enough to stare straight through a small window, into the back of the building.

A human with dark curly hair and glasses was cracking eggs into a metal bowl.

"There's a man in there," Tracker said to the others.

After adding each egg, the human stirred

well with an electric mixer. While Tracker watched, he added a whole carton of eggs, along with the cherries, chocolate morsels, and vanilla-bean scrapings that the beagle puppy had been smelling.

"It's the Pearsons' angel food cake recipe, all right!" Tracker said.

The man stopped stirring for a moment.

He glanced out the window . . . and his eyes met the beagle's!

"Hey, you . . . mutt!" the man thundered. "Get off my truck!"

He stamped over to the door and flung it open.

He'd picked up a large wooden spoon, and he looked ready to use it on Tracker!

"Run!" Fritz yelped.

The shepherd puppy took his own advice and hightailed it along Northville Road toward home.

CHAPTER FIVE

"Jump down, Tracker!" Jake urged. "I'll hold off the human for you!"

The Lab puppy stalked toward the man, his fangs showing and his tail held stiff.

"Hurry, Tracker!" said Sheena.

What about Mr. Purr? Tracker asked himself, glancing from the muffin man to the tarp and back again.

The human was big, and angry, and close. The orange cat was probably safe, hidden under the tarp—safer than Tracker was!

Wham! The muffin man slammed the spoon down hard on the truck roof. Tracker dodged it.

I'll bring the Pearsons back for Mr. Purr. Then they'll smell our recipe, too! the beagle thought.

He gathered himself to leap . . .

"More puppies! Where did they come from? Did the Animal Control van spring a leak?" the muffin man rumbled.

He swung at Tracker again with the wooden spoon, just missing him.

Sheena and Rosie yapped at the muffin man and circled him furiously, whirling like runaway tops.

"These two must be loony!" the human muttered. He swatted at the girls with his spoon. "Get . . . out . . . of . . . here, do you hear me!"

Growling, Jake grabbed the bottom of the man's trouser leg with his strong teeth and tugged.

"Cut that out!" the muffin man shouted at the Lab puppy. He grazed Jake's shoulder with the spoon.

Jake yelped and danced away from him. Sheena and Rosie scooted away from the human, too.

But Tracker's three friends had given him enough time to hop safely from the top of the truck to the hood to the ground.

"I'm down!" Tracker barked. "Thanks, guys."

"Watch out, here he comes!" Sheena yipped.

The human was hurtling toward the beagle puppy, wooden spoon raised high to whack him.

"Beat feet!" Tracker said to the others.

The four puppies scattered like ants, leaving the angry human to wave his wooden spoon and bluster.

Tracker, Jake, Sheena, and Rosie ran as fast as they could. They didn't slow down until they'd traveled the whole length of

Northville Road. When they reached the corner of Oak Street, they finally felt safe enough to stop.

Panting, tongues hanging out, the four puppies collapsed in a heap under a shady tree.

"Definitely the Pearsons' recipe," said Tracker when he got some of his breath back.

Jake licked his shoulder where the spoon had landed. "That muffin man has one nasty temper."

"I'll have to figure out how to get the Pearsons over there," said Tracker. "They'll deal with the man, human to human."

"And what about poor old Mr. Purr?" Sheena said. "The Pearsons could be in the city for hours."

Rosie added, "By then, it might be too late."

The four puppies shook their heads, not wanting to imagine what might happen to the big orange cat. They'd had their disagreements with him, but he was a part of their lives.

"I'm croaking with thirst," Sheena murmured at last.

"Come into the bakery. The Pearsons filled two water bowls for me before they

44

left," Tracker said.

The puppies trudged across the parking lot, dog-tired.

Tracker was climbing the steps when the back door of the bakery flew open: it was the Pearsons, back from the city already! And they didn't look pleased.

Jake noticed their expressions, too. "Uh-oh," he said, backing away.

"I have to get home before Heather comes for lunch," Sheena said quickly.

"Yeah, later, Tracker," said Rosie.

The three of them hustled off, leaving the beagle to face his humans.

"Tracker, where have you been?" Mr. Pearson said sternly to the puppy at his feet.

"You've worried us half to death!" said Mrs. Pearson.

But she gave Tracker a hug.

"First we spotted Fritz racing down Main Street as if a bear were chasing him," she went on. "Then we walked into the bakery and found Puffy really upset about something.

He's been yowling at the top of his lungs."

Tracker could hear the cat howling inside.

"He's a nervous wreck, and Mr. Purr is nowhere around," Mr. Pearson said. "When we discovered that you weren't here, either . . ."

". . . we didn't know *what* to think!" said Mrs. Pearson. "You're panting, and all worn out. You and your friends haven't been chasing Mr. Purr, have you?"

The puppies had been known to bother the cats.

"Plus, our angel food cake recipe is missing off the refrigerator," Mr. Pearson said. "Luckily, I know it by heart."

Which made Tracker feel a little better.

Mr. Pearson added, "I'm not blaming you, Tracker. But could Jake or Sheena or Rosie have eaten it?"

To be accused of eating the recipe, after all the help they'd been to Tracker? The beagle barked indignantly.

"He's trying to tell us something, Fred,"

Mrs. Pearson said. "Aren't you, boy?"

Tracker leaped off the steps and raced across the parking lot toward the street, yipping excitedly. Then he dashed back to where the Pearsons were standing.

Mr. Pearson said, "You want us to follow you?"

"Is that it, Tracker?" said Mrs. Pearson.

Tracker yelped his answer.

"All right, we're coming," Mrs. Pearson said, heading out into the parking lot herself.

But Tracker didn't think the Pearsons would want to *walk* all the way to the Muffin Man. It was far, and it would take too long. By the time they got there, Mr. Purr could be . . .

Or what if they had to carry the heavy cat all the way home?

The Pearsons' truck was parked next to a tree on the far side of the lot. Tracker ran over to it and scratched at the door on the driver's side.

"Look, Fred—he is so smart!" Mrs.

Pearson said proudly.

"He certainly is. We'll get in the truck, boy," Mr. Pearson told him.

"You can show us where you want us to go," said Mrs. Pearson.

You two are pretty smart yourselves! Tracker thought, wagging his tail gratefully.

CHAPTER SIX

As tired as he was, Tracker led the Pearsons all the way up Northville Road, trotting along the edge of the blacktop.

Not that they didn't try to talk him out of it.

Every few minutes, Mrs. Pearson yelled to him from the truck, "Tracker, sweetie, aren't you exhausted?"

"Why don't you get in here with us, and we'll drive you straight back to the bakery for a snack and a nap," Mr. Pearson suggested.

Which sounded wonderful. But Tracker had been left in charge that morning, and

he'd messed up the job. Now maybe he could fix it.

At last, the smell of muffins and coffee tickled his nose. The beagle puppy stopped short about half a block from the Muffin Man. Tracker sat down on the grassy shoulder of the road to let the Pearsons know they should stop, too.

Mr. Pearson steered the truck onto the

grass. "What's next?" Tracker heard him say to his wife.

"Surely Mr. Purr wouldn't have wandered this far from home," Mrs. Pearson said.

She called, "Tracker, are you ready to come with us?"

Tracker barked urgently.

"No, he wants us to get out, Fred," Mrs. Pearson said.

"Do we really believe we can read that puppy's mind?" Mr. Pearson said grumpily. But he opened his door.

As soon as both of his humans climbed out of the truck, Tracker crossed Northville Road. He glanced over his shoulder every few steps, to encourage them to follow.

"Fred, he's leading us to the Muffin Man," Mrs. Pearson said.

"I stopped by here for an iced coffee a couple of days ago," said Mr. Pearson. "Mike and I talked about the bake-off, and he told me that he's thinking about selling fancy baked goods himself, to some of the restaurants around Buxton."

And that's when he got the idea to steal your cake recipe! Tracker thought.

The beagle puppy paused in front of the small building and raised his nose high. The air around him was flooded with the rich scents of a freshly baked cherry-chocolate-chip angel food cake!

"There! Don't you smell it?" he barked to his humans. "It's *your cake!*"

But they seemed to have nonworking noses.

Mrs. Pearson was saying, "The Muffin Man isn't open yet. And I can't imagine what Mr. Purr would be doing here anyway."

"Tracker's probably hungry, and he smelled muffins, not the cat. Let's go, boy." Mr. Pearson reached for the puppy's collar. "Into the truck with you."

But the beagle yapped and held his ground.

"We've come all this way, Fred. Why don't

we see where Tracker's leading us, just to make sure?" Mrs. Pearson told her husband.

Tracker wagged his tail to let her know she was making the right choice.

They circled the building, the humans calling, "Purr? Mr. Purr!"

Then the narrow back door creaked open.

Mike the muffin man stood just inside the threshold, gripping the big wooden spoon!

As soon as he saw the Pearsons, he stepped outside and quickly slammed the door closed behind him.

"Fred!" Mike almost shouted. "And Mary."

He was fidgety, and his eyes darted here and there.

Of course he's nervous, Tracker was thinking. *He just finished baking our cake!*

"Why, hello, Mike," Mr. Pearson said.

"What's going on?" said the muffin man.

"We've lost one of our cats," Mrs. Pearson replied.

"No cats around here," Mike said. "Or customers, either."

Tracker growled, deep in his throat.

"Tracker, *no!*" Mrs. Pearson said, surprised. "I don't know what's gotten into him. He's usually so friendly," she apologized.

Mike scowled at the beagle puppy. He tapped his own leg with the wooden spoon, to let Tracker know that he recognized him.

"Is that your dog?" Mike said. "Cute."

All at once there was a faint cry.

"Do you hear something?" Mrs. Pearson said.

"No," said Mike. "I'm kind of busy, so if you'll excuse me . . ."

Tracker was already trotting toward the dark truck. He pawed at the tailgate.

The Pearsons hurried over to the truck, too.

Mr. Pearson lifted a corner of the plastic tarp . . .

"Well, I'll be! It's Mr. Purr, just like Tracker has been trying to tell us!" he exclaimed.

CHAPTER SEVEN

"Good boy, Tracker!" Mrs. Pearson said. "Are you all right, Mr. Purr?" she added worriedly, stroking the cat's fat side.

"He's not looking too perky," Mr. Pearson said, sounding uneasy himself.

Mr. Purr meowed again, a little louder and stronger this time.

"His front foot is bleeding. And he has a big lump on his head," Mr. Pearson said. "Here—I'll lift him out."

When he scooped Mr. Purr up, the cat squeaked in pain.

"We'll take him straight to Dr. Soboroff!" said Mrs. Pearson. Dr. Soboroff was the

veterinarian who doctored the two orange cats, and all of the puppies as well.

"But how did Mr. Purr ever end up here?" Mrs. Pearson wondered. She turned to Mike. "This is a long way from the Main Street Bakery."

Mike was quick. "You know, I was parked on Main Street early this morning," he said. "I was picking up my workboots at Scott's Shoe Repair, so I was only a couple of doors down from your bakery. Your cat must have jumped into my truck to poke around, he crawled under the tarp, and . . ."

Mike reached out to pat Mr. Purr, pretending he liked animals. But he jerked his hand back fast, because there was a yowl and a hiss.

Tracker was glad to know that the orange cat had some fight left!

"Since you couldn't see Mr. Purr under the tarp, you drove away with him," Mr. Pearson finished for Mike.

"That's right. He might have bumped his head bouncing around back there," said the muffin man.

"I'm just happy we found him," said Mr. Pearson.

"Actually, Tracker found him," Mrs. Pearson pointed out. "I wonder how this puppy knew exactly where Mr. Purr was . . . ."

She glanced at Mike out of the corner of her eye—he was glaring at the beagle.

"Well, we're off to the vet's," Mr. Pearson was saying. He headed toward his truck on the far side of Northville Road, the heavy cat cradled in his arms.

"Yes, goodbye, Mike," Mrs. Pearson said.

She looked straight at the big wooden spoon in his hand, and picked up Tracker, tucking him safely under her arm.

As they hurried after Mr. Pearson and Mr. Purr, Mike called, "I'm entering the bake-off at the food fair!"

"The more the merrier!" Mr. Pearson called back.

Dr. Soboroff said that Mr. Purr had gotten a nasty knock on his head, he was bruised all over, and two of the nails on his left front foot were missing.

"He probably tore them off trying to hang onto the truck," the veterinarian told the Pearsons. "But nails grow back."

He added, "Mr. Purr will have a headache for a few days. He should take it easy for a while."

"He won't leave the bakery," Mrs. Pearson promised.

"We'll be getting ready for the big bake-off at the fairgrounds," Mr. Pearson said. "We won't let him out of our sight."

They weren't going to let Tracker run around town, either.

"We don't want to have to worry about this puppy, not with cakes to make," Mr. Pearson told his wife when they got back to the Main Street Bakery.

Mrs. Pearson said, "I'll certainly feel better knowing exactly where *all* of our animals are. I'm still not certain how or why Mr. Purr ended up at the Muffin Man, or how Tracker knew he was there. That Mike seemed a little shifty to me. . . ."

Tracker was stuck at the bakery.

But Sheena, Rosie, Jake, and Fritz could visit him there. They showed up early the next morning, and snacked on puppy-bites of almond croissants, served by the Pearsons on the back steps.

Tracker's humans were working away inside the bakery: cake pans clanked, the new electric mixer whirred, oven doors opened and closed, timers rang.

All the noise in the world wouldn't have bothered Mr. Purr. He was sleeping off his adventure, snoring away in the side window.

But every few minutes one or the other of the Pearsons peered out to the steps, to make sure their puppy was where he was supposed to be.

"So tomorrow's the big bake-off," Sheena said to Tracker, her mouth stuffed full of flaky pastry and crushed almonds.

"Then everything's back to normal, right?" said Fritz.

The German shepherd puppy liked "normal" a lot more than "exciting" or "different."

"Normal?" said the beagle. "What if Mike beats the Pearsons with their own recipe? If Mike wins, nothing will ever be normal for me again."

Just thinking about it made him grind his puppy teeth. "If I'd stayed here instead of going to the park . . ."

"What could you have done against a big, mean human like Mike?" said Rosie. "You're just a puppy."

"And he's scary!" Fritz said breathlessly.

"Of course, if *all* of us had stayed here with you—" Jake said.

"Listen, I have a plan," Tracker interrupted. "Both of the Pearsons will be busy at the bake-off tomorrow, so they won't be able to keep an eye on me. I'll sneak over to the fairgrounds, and—"

"No, *we'll* sneak over there," Jake corrected him.

"Absolutely," said Rosie.

"Right," said Sheena.

Fritz whimpered, but he nodded his head, both ears flopping loosely.

"Thanks. So *we'll* sneak over there, we'll track Mike down, and we'll . . . stop him!" said Tracker.

"Is that really a plan?" Sheena wondered.

Maybe not. But that was as far as Tracker had gotten.

CHAPTER EIGHT

It was late in the evening when the Pearsons were finally satisfied. The cake they chose for the bake-off was the tallest and lightest and moistest.

Mrs. Pearson had covered it with chocolate icing and lots and lots of cherries.

It looked beautiful, and it smelled even better.

Tracker licked his lips just thinking about how it must taste.

"We'll bring home the grand-prize trophy with this one, no question!" Mr. Pearson said to his wife as they admired

their cherry-chocolate-chip angel food cake. "If everything goes well."

"And what could go wrong, with such a gorgeous creation?" Mrs. Pearson said proudly.

Plenty, Tracker was thinking, since Mike had the exact same recipe.

The Pearsons packed their masterpiece in a large cake box, careful not to mash the decorations. They slid the box into the shiny steel refrigerator, and took off their aprons.

"Job well done. Let's go home and get some sleep," Mr. Pearson said.

"I'll carry Mr. Purr," said Mrs. Pearson.

"I'll bring Puffy," said Mr. Pearson.

The orange cats stayed at the bakery most weeknights, keeping at least one eye open for mice.

But Mr. Purr was so bumped and bruised that he'd be sleeping on the Pearsons' soft bed at night for some time.

Puffy's nerves were still shot. He'd been spending the day huddled in the broom closet, and the Pearsons didn't want to leave him behind.

They picked up both cats and turned off the lights in the shop. With Tracker at their heels, they headed out the door into the empty parking lot.

No one glanced at what was left of the old building across the way. If anyone had, he might have noticed dozens of pairs of tiny eyes glinting in the shadows.

The mice were ready to make their move.

As soon as the Pearsons' truck rolled through the exit onto Oak Street, a gang of rodents scampered toward the back of

the Main Street Bakery.

Tracker spent a troubled night on his pillow on the Pearsons' bedroom floor. He dreamed that Mike had chased him into the animal shelter with a gigantic wooden spoon.

Mr. Purr growled and hissed in his sleep, and Puffy twitched and trembled on top of the chest of drawers.

The humans tossed and turned restlessly, too.

"I'm still tired," Mr. Pearson said as he unlocked the door at the bakery the next morning.

"I just hope everything goes smoothly today," Mrs. Pearson added.

When the family stepped inside the back room, however, Tracker's hair stood on end—the whole place reeked of mice!

They'd gnawed small, round holes in the bags of flour and sugar and cornmeal. Flour-dusted mouse tracks trailed up and down the aisles, over the counters, and crisscrossed the

71

stove. Most of the bottles had been knocked out of the spice racks. Boxes of raisins and apricots and plums had been torn open, and the dried fruit was scattered from one end of the back room to the other.

Mr. Purr yowled angrily from Mr. Pearson's arms.

"Oh, Fred!" Mrs. Pearson exclaimed. "What a horrible mess!"

She was clutching Puffy. As soon as she

put him down, the cat scuttled under the stove . . . and three mice dashed out, to disappear behind a bag of pecans.

"I'll call 911 Exterminator," Mr. Pearson said grimly, setting Mr. Purr down, too. "People will not buy anything from a bakery riddled with mice, no matter how many trophies we win."

"But it's a summer weekend. I'm sure the exterminator is closed until Monday," Mrs. Pearson said. "I'll stay here and set traps and start cleaning."

"No, *you* go to the bake-off, and I'll handle this," Mr. Pearson said. "Tracker will help me."

There went the beagle's last chance to make things right about Mike and the stolen recipe. But if his humans needed him for mouse patrol . . . The puppy raced over to a bag of cornmeal and flushed out a large brown mouse with a snap of his teeth.

Then Mrs. Pearson said, "Fred, why

can't we leave the animals here to frighten the mice away from the stove, and out of the front room, maybe even shoo a few through the dog door. We'll both go to the bake-off, and clean up when we get back."

"I guess we could leave the bakery closed for the whole day," said Mr. Pearson, nodding.

"Good. We'd better hurry—at least our cake was safe in here!" Mrs. Pearson said, opening the refrigerator.

"I'll grab a fancy plate for it," said her husband. "Tracker, you're in charge while we're gone."

By the time Jake, Sheena, and Rosie slid through the dog door that morning, Tracker had run for miles already, hunting mice inside the bakery.

"Wow—I've never smelled so many rodents in one place at one time!" Jake said excitedly, sniffing the air.

"This could be as much fun as chasing

water rats at the lake!" said Rosie.

She snarled at a couple of plump gray mice lurking under the refrigerator.

"Rats at the lake are okay. Rats in our houses are definitely not," Sheena said, wrinkling her nose. She bounced a medium-sized black mouse out from behind a cabinet.

"So when do we leave for the fairgrounds to find Mike?" Jake asked Tracker.

"We don't," the beagle told him. "The Pearsons expect me to take care of the place. And this time I will."

"Why can't the cats do it?" said Rosie. "Aren't mice *their* job?"

"Puffy's hiding in the front room," Tracker said. "And Mr. Purr is so banged up he can hardly move."

"Hey, I'm the best mouser in town!" the orange cat argued from his bed on a bag of cornmeal. But he groaned when he tried to scramble to his feet.

"See? There's nothing I can do about

that cheating muffin man," Tracker said sadly.

So Fritz surprised everyone when he stuck his head through the dog door and woofed, "I'll do it!"

"You'll do what, Fritzie?" Sheena said.

"I'll stay here and chase mice," Fritz said.

"Get real!" Mr. Purr muttered.

Tracker knew what he meant: Fritz might be the biggest of the puppies, and the strongest, but he certainly wasn't the bravest, not even against mice.

Rosie said, "Then the rest of us could go to the fairgrounds and find that cake burglar!"

"Let me try, Tracker!" Fritz said. His bark was sounding deeper and a little more grown-up.

"His size alone will scare mice away," Sheena whispered to Tracker. "Give him a chance."

Tracker wanted so badly to help the

Pearsons win the bake-off.

"Okay!" he said at last.

"Excellent!" said Jake, Rosie, and Sheena.

"I'll do a good job, Tracker," Fritz said, and his drooping ear straightened up for a second. "If you guys will help me squeeze through this dog door . . ."

CHAPTER NINE

A few minutes later, Tracker was racing up Main Street with his friends. They cut through yards, over to Lilac Avenue, where Sheena and Fritz's houses were, onto Middle Road. They ran until they reached the York County Fairgrounds.

The fairgrounds were jammed with cars and trucks and people. Colorful banners flapped in the wind above several huge tents.

The puppies pressed through the crowds and crawled under the hem of the first tent. It was bursting with displays of shiny pots and pans, baking sheets, electric choppers, blenders, and mixers—everything a cook

might possibly need.

Gleaming stoves and refrigerators were lined up in the second tent.

Finally the four puppies popped up inside the tent where the entries for the bake-off had been set up. A dozen long tables were loaded down with pies and cookies. And cakes: chocolate cakes, vanilla cakes, strawberry cakes, upside-down cakes, pound cakes.

"It smells heavenly in here!" Sheena said.

"Yeah, and I'm starved!" said Jake.

"I'm drooling," Rosie said.

"Keep your minds on Mike," Tracker told them.

As they edged around a large group of chattering humans, he added, "Does anybody see him? And look out for the Pearsons, too." The last thing the beagle puppy wanted was for his people to spot him before he'd finished his job.

It was hard to see anything at all, actually, because there were so many legs in the way—human legs, chair legs, and table legs.

Jake was taking a good, hard look at a whipped-cream cake when a woman with a name tag on her shirt thundered, "No dogs allowed in here!"

The four puppies scurried under a table draped with a long tablecloth. They kept out of sight while they sniffed the air for a particular cake, and sniffed at feet for a certain human.

All at once, Rosie said, "Psst . . . Tracker! Here's Mr. Pearson!"

Even without human scents to prove it, the puppies would have recognized the shoes beneath the table: Mr. Pearson always wore those leather clogs when he cooked, and Mrs. Pearson's canvas hightops were right beside them. Wafting down from above were the yummy smells of the cherry-chocolate-chip angel food cake.

"Let's put some space between us!" Tracker murmured to his friends.

Mike the muffin man would want to stay

far away from the Pearsons, too.

Darting under the next table, and the one after that, the puppies slowly made their way across the huge space.

Finally Tracker smelled a mix of cherries and chocolate and vanilla for the second time.

"I smell our cake again, so this has to be Mike!" the beagle puppy growled through his teeth.

"Where?" Jake rumbled. "I'd like to bite his leg, after that whack he gave me!"

"Check out those workboots," Tracker answered.

The toes of Mike's boots were tapping the floor nervously.

"What should we do now?" Sheena asked Tracker.

"We could start barking—make a scene," Rosie said, "so everyone would notice him, and the cake that he stole."

"Mike might say the Pearsons stole the recipe from *him*," Tracker pointed out.

He should have made a real plan before they'd come this far. . . .

Someone must have lifted a tent flap, because a sudden breeze filled Tracker's nose with dozens of tasty scents. The beagle puppy smelled nutmeg, and cinnamon, and ginger . . . and ginger . . .

Ginger always made him sneeze.

"*Aaa-choo!*" Tracker sneezed once, and again, "*Aaa-choo!*"

He bumped into Rosie, who stumbled over Mike's workboots.

"Wha-a-at?" a human exclaimed from above them.

Mike's head suddenly appeared under the tablecloth. "Not you mutts again!" he roared.

When he grabbed for Tracker, Mike's shoulders hit the edge of the table . . .

"Look out—it's going over!" Tracker yelped to his friends.

The table crashed to the ground, sending cakes and people every which way!

Before the puppies dashed out of the tent, Tracker made a point to jump right in the middle of Mike's cherry-chocolate-chip angel food cake! And Jake took a big bite out of the icing.

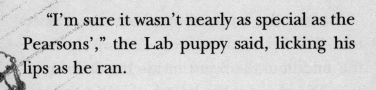

"I'm sure it wasn't nearly as special as the Pearsons'," the Lab puppy said, licking his lips as he ran.

The four puppies tore across the

fairgrounds, and galloped all the way to the bakery.

Fritz met them just inside the dog door.

"Did you do it?" he asked. "Did you get the muffin man?"

"Him *and* his stolen cake!" said Tracker, panting happily. "What about you and the mice?"

From the shelf where he was stretched out, Mr. Purr said, "This puppy did good. He ran every last mouse out of the bakery."

"Good job, Fritzie!" Sheena told the shepherd.

"You know what, Fritz? Both of your ears are standing up!" Tracker said.

"Puffy chased the mice across the parking lot," Mr. Purr went on.

Puffy was curled up on the counter. "It was just what I needed—I feel a hundred times better," he said. His whiskers raised in a toothy grin.

The five puppies were taking it easy on

the steps when the Pearsons' truck rolled up.

Mrs. Pearson climbed out with a trophy under her arm.

"We have an audience," she said to her husband.

She held the trophy high in the air—this time, it was a big golden cake on a golden stand. "We won the grand prize again!" Mrs. Pearson said.

"They can't understand all that," said Mr. Pearson.

"But they're happy for us," Mrs. Pearson said. "See? They're wagging their tails."

"We won!" Tracker said to his friends. "And we couldn't have done it without you guys."

"Would anyone like some croissants? Vanilla ice cream?" Mrs. Pearson was asking.

"I believe they understood *that*," said Mr. Pearson, because five puppy tails were wagging even harder.

ALL-AMERICAN PUPPIES

They're cute.
They're cuddly. They're frisky.
And they just can't stay out of trouble!

Don't miss any of the pups' adventures in Buxton, USA:

#1 NEW PUP ON THE BLOCK
Jake and his pals are on the loose!

#2 ON THE SCENT OF TROUBLE
Rosie and Fritz are hot on the trail!

#3 CAMP BARKALOT
A week in the wild!

#4 UPTOWN POODLE, DOWNTOWN PUPS
What's a poodle good for, anyhow?

#5 PUPPYSAURUS
The pups dig up more than trouble this time!